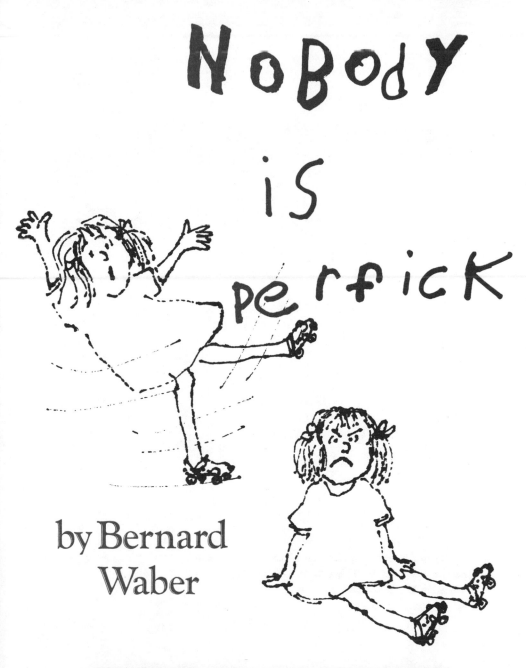

NoBodY iS perfick

by Bernard Waber

HOUGHTON MIFFLIN COMPANY BOSTON

for *SHIRA* *and* *ELYSE*

and in remembrance of *RICHARD*

NOBODY
IS
PERFICK

SAY SOMETHING NICE

Lizards!

That's
not nice.

Spiders!

Now you
stop it!

Arthur,
you had just
better stop!

Creepy things!

Crawly, creepy things!

I don't want
to hear it.

Oh, how terrible!
Stop it, Arthur!

Slimy, crawly,
creepy things!

Green, slimy, crawly, creepy things!

You're frightening me!

With beady eyes!

AR-THUR! AR-THUR!

Green, slimy, crawly,
creepy things
with beady eyes
and fangy teeth!

Oh, I can't
stand it!

And
thorny
legs!

Yilk!

Lots and lots
and lots
of thorny legs!

Oh, please!
Oh, please stop!

MONSTERS!
TERRIBLE MONSTERS
ARE COMING!
DO YOU HEAR ME?

Ooooooh!

15

THEY ARE CRAWLING
OUT OF CAVES...
RISING FROM THE SEA...
DROPPING FROM THE SKY!
MONSTERS! MONSTERS!
WE ARE SURROUNDED!

You're
so scary,
Arthur!

Harriet! Harriet!
It's time to come
in now, dear.

17

Oh! Oh! I have
to go in.
This was fun.
Let's do it again,
tomorrow.

Grrr...

THAT WAS SOME DREAM.
HA! HA! HA!

Last night . . .
ha! ha! ha!
I dreamed . . .
ha! ha! ha!
I dreamed
I was in this
strange place . . .
ha! ha! ha!

Ha! Ha! Ha!
Ha! Ha! Ha!
And in this place . . .
ha! ha! ha!
there were these . . .
ha! ha! ha!
ha! ha! ha!
purple cows . . .
ha! ha! ha!

Ha! Ha! Ha!
And these purple cows
were wearing striped . . .
ha! ha! ha!
ha! ha! ha!

Ha! Ha! Ha!
Striped what?

Ha! Ha! Ha!
Ha! Ha! Ha!
Striped . . .
ha! ha! ha!
ha! ha! ha!
ha! ha! ha!

Ha! Ha! Ha!
Ha! Ha! Ha!
Striped what?
Ha! Ha! Ha!
Ha! Ha! Ha!
Ha! Ha! Ha!

Ha! Ha! Ha!   Ha! Ha! Ha!
Ha! Ha! Ha!   Ha! Ha! Ha!
Ha! Ha! Ha!   Ha! Ha! Ha!
Ha! Ha! Ha!   Striped what?
Ha! Ha! Ha!   Ha! Ha! Ha!
Ha! Ha! Ha!   Ha! Ha! Ha!

Ha! Ha! Ha!   Ha! Ha! Ha!
Ha! Ha! Ha!   Ha! Ha! Ha!
Ha! Ha! Ha!   Ha! Ha! Ha!
Ha! Ha! Ha!   Ha! Ha! Ha!
Ha! Ha! Ha!   Ha! Ha! Ha!

It's too funny!
Ha! Ha! Ha!
Ha! Ha! Ha!
Ha! Ha! Ha!
Ha! Ha! Ha!

Tell me! Tell me!
Ha! Ha! Ha!
Ha! Ha! Ha!
Ha! Ha! Ha!
Ha! Ha! Ha!

I'll have to...
ha! ha! ha!
ha! ha! ha!
tell you...
ha! ha! ha!   Ha! Ha! Ha!
ha! ha! ha!   Ha! Ha! Ha!
later...   Ha! Ha! Ha!
ha! ha! ha!   Ha! Ha! Ha!
ha! ha! ha!   Ha! Ha! Ha!

Ha! Ha! Ha!
Ha! Ha! Ha!
Good-
ha! ha! ha!
ha! ha! ha!
bye . . .
ha! ha! ha!
ha! ha! ha!

Ha! Ha! Ha!
Ha! Ha! Ha!
Ha! Ha! Ha!
Ha! Ha! Ha!
Ha! Ha! Ha!

Ha! Ha! Ha!   Ha! Ha! Ha!
Ha! Ha! Ha!   Ha! Ha! Ha!
Ha! Ha! Ha!   Ha! Ha! Ha!
Ha! Ha! Ha!   Ha! Ha! Ha!
Ha! Ha! Ha!   Ha! Ha! Ha!

Ha! Ha! Ha!

Hmmmmmmmmm . . .

STRIPED WHAT???????

THAT WAS SOME DAYDREAM
Mmmmmmmmmmmm!

I am going
to have
a daydream.
I can feel it
coming on.

But I don't want
to have a daydream.
I really don't
want to have
a daydream.

I am pinching
myself so I
won't have a
daydream.

I am having a
glass of water
so I won't have
a daydream.

I am chewing
bubble gum
so I won't have
a daydream.

I am making
myself dizzy
so I won't have
a daydream.

I am rolling
over and over
so I won't have
a daydream.

I don't want to
have a daydream.
I really don't want
to have a daydream.

I will think about arithmetic...
and how if I have a dozen pears
and I give away seven
I would then have...

I would then have...

a daydream.

NO RAIN AGAIN TODAY

I have a new
raincoat.
See my new
raincoat.

And I have a
new rainhat.
See my new
rainhat.

And I have new
rainboots.
See my new
rainboots.

And I have a
new umbrella.
See my new
umbrella.

And I wait for rain.
I wait and wait and wait.

But every day the sun keeps shining...

and shining...

and shining...

So I can't wear
my new raincoat.

And I can't wear
my new rainhat.

And I can't wear
my new rainboots.

And I can't carry
my new umbrella.

Each night I whisper:
if only it would rain…
if only it would rain.

But in the morning
the bright sun
wakes me.

And then I know I will
have to face another
AWFUL, TERRIBLE, MISERABLE,
ROTTEN, MEAN, NASTY
beautiful new day.

MY DIARY

This is my diary.
It's very private...
and very personal.
I won't let anyone
read it.

Not even your mother?   Not even my mother.
Not even your father?   Not even my father.

May I look at it?

NO!
It's personal
and private.

May I just peek at
the color
of the
pages?

Well . . .

All right . . .
just the color
of the pages.

Please?
Oh, please?

Pink!
Oh, how
beautiful!

May I just peek
at the first word
on the first page?

NO!

Look.
I'll let you
wear my Indian
bracelet.

You will!
You really will?
Well . . .
all right, but
just the first
word on the
first page.
That's all!

There!

It says, "I."
The first word
is "I."

May I just peek
at the
second
word?
Please?

NO!
It's personal
and private.

I'll let you
feed my cat.

You will! You promise?
Well . . .
all right,
just the
second word.
And that's all.
Understand?

There!

It says, "think."
"I think . . ."

May I just peek
at the third word?

NO!

Please?
Please?
Please?

No!
No!
No!

I'll let you wear my
good-luck charm. The one
my Aunt Grace sent from
Atlantic City.

You will!

All right . . .
just the third word.
**AND THAT'S ALL!
THAT IS ALL!
UNDERSTAND!**

There!

It says, "David."
"I think David . . ."

I'll let you dress
my baby sister.

ALL RIGHT...
just the fourth word.
And that's the last!
LAST! LAST! LAST!

It says, "is."
"I think David is . . ."
Is what?

I can't tell you.

It's not fair.
"Is" is such a little word.
It's hardly a word at all.
It shouldn't have counted
as a word.

Please, may I
see the fifth word?
Please?   NO!
Please?
PLEASE?

If you won't let me
see the fifth word,
I won't be your friend.

You won't?
You mean it?

There!
There's the
fifth word.

It says, "nice."
"I think David is nice."

Do you really?
Do you really
think David
is nice?

Uh-huh.

SITTING UP STRAIGHT

In the beginning
I always sit up
straight.
Like this.

See how I sit
up straight.
Straight as a
poker, I sit.

And I keep
remembering to
sit up straight.
That's because
I tell myself
to sit up
straight.

I say to myself,
"You are to sit
up straight. Hear?
Now don't you forget
it. Remember now,
sit up straight.
Sit up straight!
Sit up straight!!"

And then it happens.
When does it happen?
I begin to forget
I am supposed to
remember to sit up
straight.

And I keep
forgetting . . .

and forgetting . . .

and forgetting . . .

and forgetting . . .

to sit up straight.

Suddenly, my teacher
says, "You are slumping.
Sit up straight!"

And then I have
to begin all over
again . . .

to remember
to sit up straight . . .
to sit up straight . . .
to sit up straight.

TEN BEST

Ten best what?

Ten best days
of the year.

Are there only ten?

There are only
ten best.

Well, first, of course, there
is my birthday. And then
there is Christmas, Easter,
Halloween, Thanksgiving, July 4th,
my mother's birthday, my father's
birthday, the first day of spring,

What
are
they?

and the
first day
of summer . . .
in that
order.

97

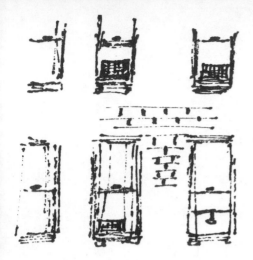

How about the first
day of winter? You can
make a snowman on the
first day of winter . . .
sometimes.

I know.

Then why don't you add
the first day of winter
to your list? Isn't
that a good idea?

I can't.

Because that would
make eleven. You
can't have eleven
on a ten-best list.

Why
not?

Then why don't you change
it to an eleven-best list?
Isn't that a good idea?

I can't.

Why not?

Because I will have to
change all of my other
ten-best lists to
eleven best.

I have lots of other lists.
It's one of the ten best
things I like to do:
make lists.

You
have
other
lists?

Let me see . . .
well, first I have my
ten-best-friends-of-
the-year list.

What kinds
of lists?

And then I have my
ten best colors,
ten best things to do,
ten best television programs,
ten best games,
ten best songs,
ten best books,
ten best ice cream flavors,
ten best things I want
to be when I grow up,
and ten best ways to fall
asleep on a hot night.

Why...   do you...

make lists?

So I will
know what
the ten
best are,
silly.

Did you
call me
silly?

You asked a
silly question.

You're the one
who is silly,
if you want to
know.
YOU'RE REAL
SILLY!

You're
sillier!

You're sillier!
You're the silliest
person I ever met
in my whole life!
That's how
silly you are.

Just for that
I'm going to cross
you off of my ten-
best-friends-of-the-
year list!

Yes, you were.
But now, I'm going
to cross you off.

Was I on your
ten-best-friends-
of-the-year list?
Was I really?

I'll put Doris
Dinkerhoffer in
your place.
GOOD-BYE!!!

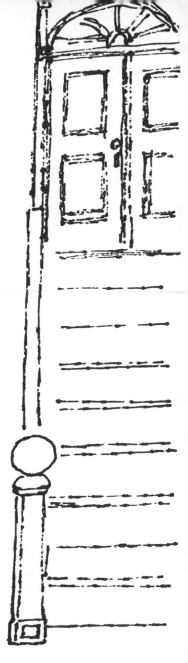

Oh, who cares about her
silly old list anyway?

Yes, who cares?

PETER PERFECT

The Story of a Perfect Boy

Your name is Peter Perfect
and you are the perfect boy.

PLEASE

THANK YOU

EXCUSE ME

I BEG YOUR PARDON

YES, SIR

NO, SIR

YOU'RE VERY WELCOME

TO BE SURE

Your mother is proud of you.

MY SON, PETER, IS THE PERFECT BOY.
I NEVER HAVE A MOMENT'S TROUBLE WITH HIM.
HE EATS EVERYTHING.
HE IS WONDERFUL.

More, please.

Does he eat raw eggs?

He loves them.

Raw eggs! Yilk!!

Your father is proud of you.

MY SON, PETER, IS MORE
THAN WONDERFUL.
HE IS PERFECT.

What is
more than
perfect? Superperfect?

Maybe.

Your teacher is proud of you.

PETER PERFECT ALWAYS SITS UP STRAIGHT.
PETER PERFECT IS NEVER ABSENT OR LATE.
PETER PERFECT IS ALWAYS HELPFUL.
PETER PERFECT NEVER DAYDREAMS.
PETER PERFECT ALWAYS COMES PREPARED
WITH A SHARP PENCIL.

This morning
I had a pencil
with a point.
Now, I have
a pencil without
a point.

Does that
make you
pointless?

People, everywhere, are talking about you, Peter Perfect.

"DID YOU KNOW THAT PETER PERFECT HAS NEVER...

RIPPED HIS PANTS
SLURPED MILK

GIGGLED IN CLASS
TRIPPED OVER HIS OWN FEET
BROKEN A TOY

LEANED ON HIS ELBOW
STUCK OUT HIS TONGUE

TALKED WITH HIS MOUTH FULL
SLAMMED A DOOR
INTERRUPTED WHEN OTHERS SPEAK

SCUFFED HIS SHOES
PASSED A NOTE
OR LOST SO MUCH AS A GLOVE?"

I am looking
for a glove.

Has anyone seen my glove?

Sorry.

It's brown,
with green
polka dots...
and a hole in
the thumb.

Mothers make an example of you.

WHY CAN'T YOU BE LIKE PETER
PERFECT? PETER PERFECT WOULD
NEVER EAT SPAGHETTI WITH HIS
FINGERS. NOT PETER PERFECT!

'WHEN MY SON, PETER PERFECT, TAKES A BATH, I NEVER HAVE TO REMIND HIM TO SCRUB BEHIND HIS EARS.' His Mother

Peter Perfect's mother never has to raise her voice.

How does he know when she means it?

'PETER PERFECT HAS PERFECT
MANNERS. HE NEVER DROPS CRUMBS
ON HIS LAP.' HIS GRANDMOTHER

You have
crumbs on
your lap.

They are
only little
crumbs.

This is my fifth straw already.

They just don't make straws the way they used to.

Have you
seen my
glove?

Sorry.

It's a
rightie.

I always
seem to lose
righties.

It's the
third rightie
I've lost
this winter.

Have you
tried
lost and
found?

See, I am
wearing two
lefties;
two different
colored
lefties.

'PETER PERFECT SLEEPS WITHOUT A NIGHTLIGHT.' His Grandfather

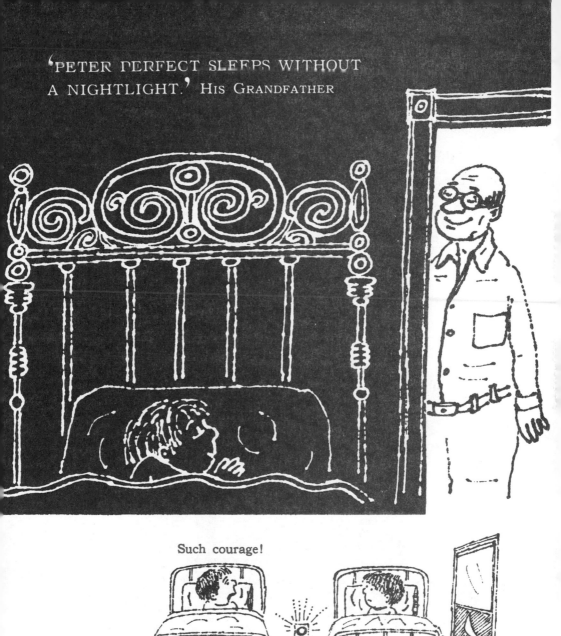

Such courage!

How about extrafine superperfect with stars and A pluses?

Maybe.

'PETER PERFECT IS PERFECT BECAUSE I RAISED HIM PERFECTLY.'

HIS FATHER

Say three
times, fast:
PETER PERFECT'S
PAPA PICKED A
PERFECT PETER!

Peter rerfic's pata
ricked da ferfic reeter!

Perter Perfect's popper
picked a perfect peeper!

Peter perpic's papa
pockta perpic peeta!

If only you were real,

Peter Perfect!